# Bubba and Beau
## Go Night-Night

Kathi Appelt          Arthur Howard

**Harcourt, Inc.**
*San Diego     New York     London*

*For my sweet brother-in-law Harry, who knows how to come to the rescue—K. A.*

Requests for permission to make copies of any part of the work should be mailed to the following address:
Permissions Department, Harcourt, Inc., 6277 Sea Harbor Drive, Orlando, Florida 32887-6777.

www.HarcourtBooks.com

Library of Congress Cataloging-in-Publication Data
Appelt, Kathi, 1954–
Bubba and Beau go night-night/by Kathi Appelt; illustrated by Arthur Howard.
p. cm.
Summary: Even after a long day of running errands, baby Bubba and his puppy Beau are not ready for bedtime.
[1. Babies—Fiction. 2. Dogs—Fiction. 3. Bedtime—Fiction.] I. Howard, Arthur, ill. II. Title.
PZ7.A6455Bv 2003
[E]—dc21 2002006311
ISBN 0-15-204593-7

First edition
H G F E D C B A

**Printed in Singapore**

The display type was set in Cloister Oldstyle Bold.
The text type was set in Cloister Oldstyle.
Color separations by Bright Arts Ltd., Hong Kong
Printed and bound by Tien Wah Press, Singapore
This book was printed on totally chlorine-free Enso Stora Matte paper.
Production supervision by Sandra Grebenar and Ginger Boyer
Designed by Arthur Howard and Judythe Sieck

# Chapter One

Bubba and Beau loved to go bye-bye.

Whenever Big Bubba went to town,
he packed those two up in his trusty
pickup, Earl, and off they went.

*Toot! Toot!* went Earl.
"Yeehaw!" yelled Big Bubba.
"Arooooo!" bayed Beau.
"Wheeeee!" squealed Bubba.

"Bye-bye!" called Mama Pearl.

Big Bubba set the radio on KBOB
and sang along with the music.
Sister, it was down the road again.

## Chapter Two

First, they went to the Feed and Seed.
Big Bubba bought corn for the chickens,
mulch for the garden,

a Bone-a-Fide chew toy for Beau,
and a pickled egg for Bubba.

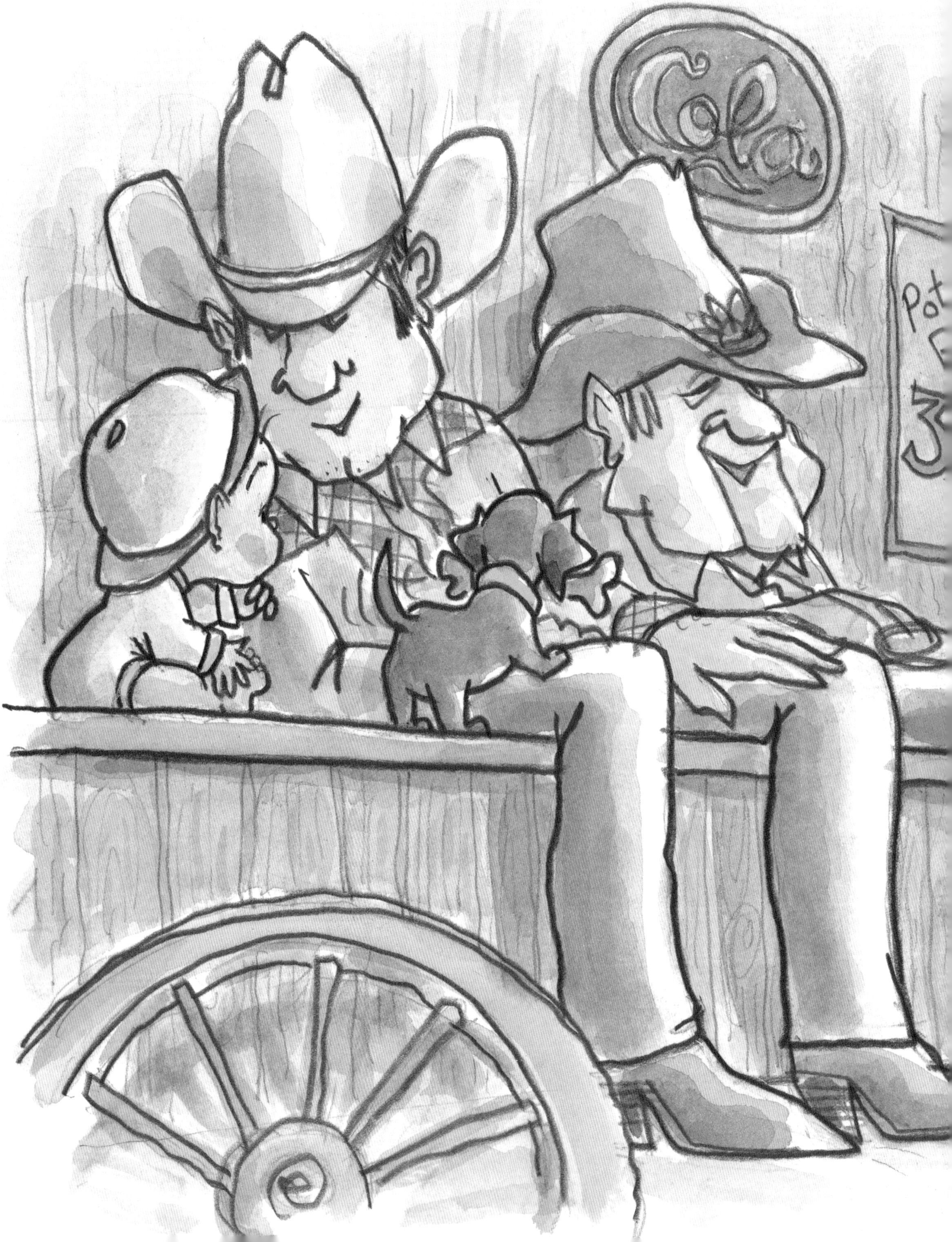
Cola

Then they sat on the front porch with their neighbors.

"Good day to shoot the breeze," said Big Bubba.

"Yep," said Jim Bob.

"Yes siree," said Roy Bob.

Billy Bob chewed on his toothpick.

It didn't take long for the breeze to be fully shot.
"Bye-bye," said Jim Bob.
"Bye-bye," said Roy Bob.
Billy Bob chewed another toothpick.

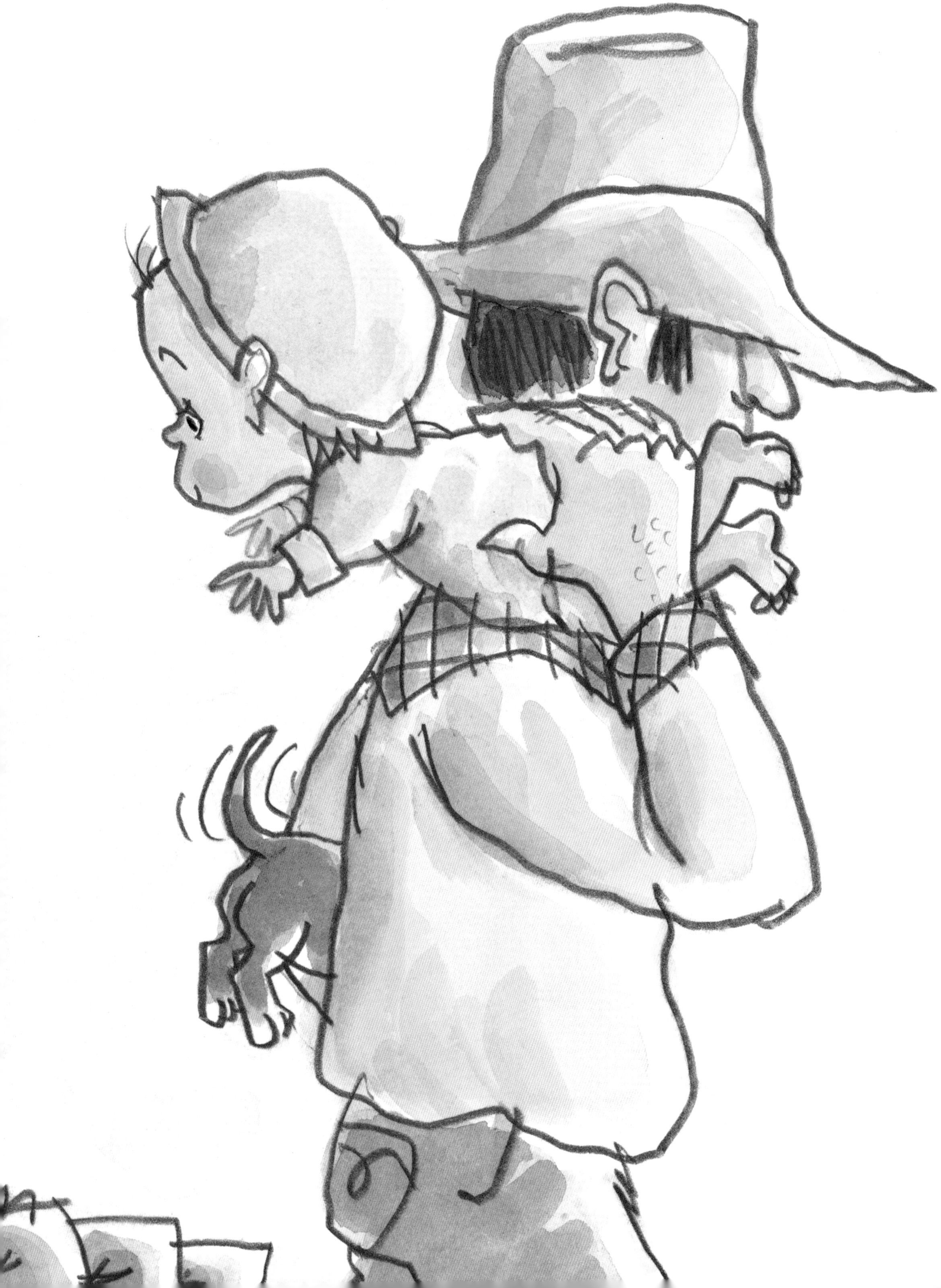

# Chapter Three

Next stop was the post office.
Big Bubba bought a roll of first-class stamps
from Mrs. Bancroft, the postmistress. Each
stamp had a picture of the American flag.

Those stamps got Big Bubba all choked up.
He stopped in his tracks and saluted.
Beau stood up on his hind legs.
Bubba squealed, "Wheeeee!"

"Bye-bye," waved Mrs. Bancroft.

After that, they went to Sam's
vegetable and fruit stand.
There were watermelons galore. Big watermelons,
little watermelons, and gigantic watermelons.

Big Bubba thumped each of them.
"It's gotta have the right sound," he said.

Bubba and Beau thumped watermelons, too.

They thumped

and thumped

and thumped.

Finally, they found just the right one.
"Bye-bye," said Sam.
Bubba waved his hand. Beau wagged his tail.
It was a happy day in Bubbaland.

# Chapter Four

Only one stop left: the Freezee Deluxe.
Big Bubba steered Earl up to the drive-thru window.
Claudine smiled from inside. "What'll it be?"

Big Bubba ordered three
raspberry-swirl ice-cream
cones and extra napkins.

Sister, those napkins came in handy.

"Bye-bye," said Claudine.
*Toot! Toot!* went Earl.
Big Bubba cranked up the radio, and they headed on home.
Yep, going bye-bye was better than butter on toast.

# Chapter Five

After such a long day, everybody was pooped.
Big Bubba stretched and yawned.
Mama Pearl stretched and yawned.

Then she looked at Bubba and Beau and said,
"Time to go night-night."

Bubba did not like to go night-night.
Beau did not like to go night-night.

No siree, Bob! Going night-night was *not* the first order of business.

# Chapter Six

Mama Pearl tried everything.
She tried rocking.

She tried warm milk.

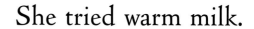

She tried singing
"Hush, Little Bubba."

Nothing worked.

Just when she thought her wits might fly right on
out the window, Big Bubba came to the rescue.
"Let's go bye-bye," he said.

He buckled Bubba and Beau into Earl
and off they went.
They drove past the Feed and Seed.
It was all shuttered up.
They drove past the post office. It was dark as could be.
They drove past Sam's vegetable and fruit stand.
All the watermelons were locked away.

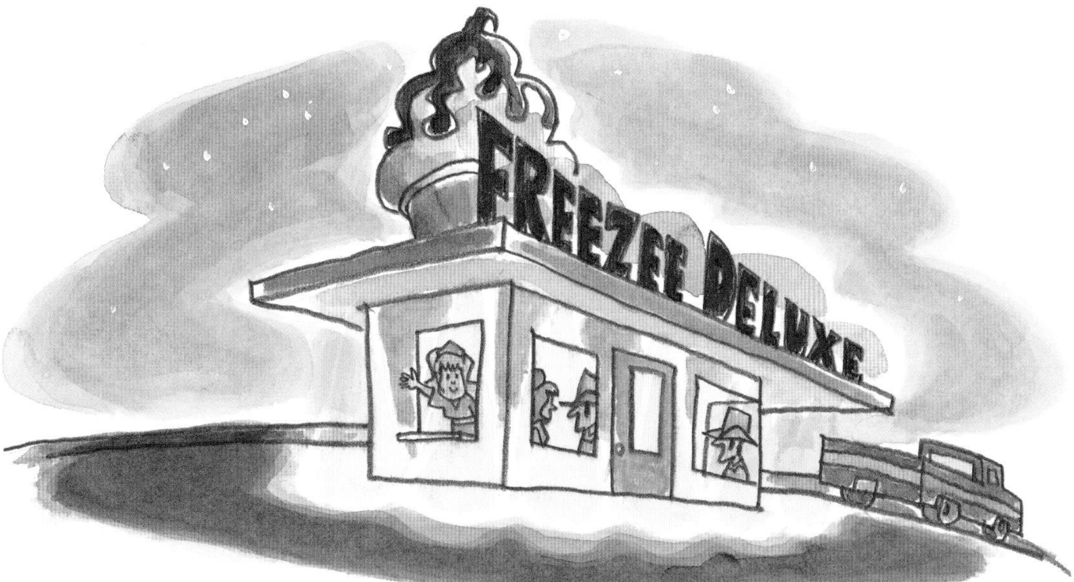
FREEZEE DELUXE

Finally, they passed the Freezee Deluxe.
Claudine waved as they rambled by.

But Bubba and Beau didn't notice.
Sister, those two were plumb tuckered out.

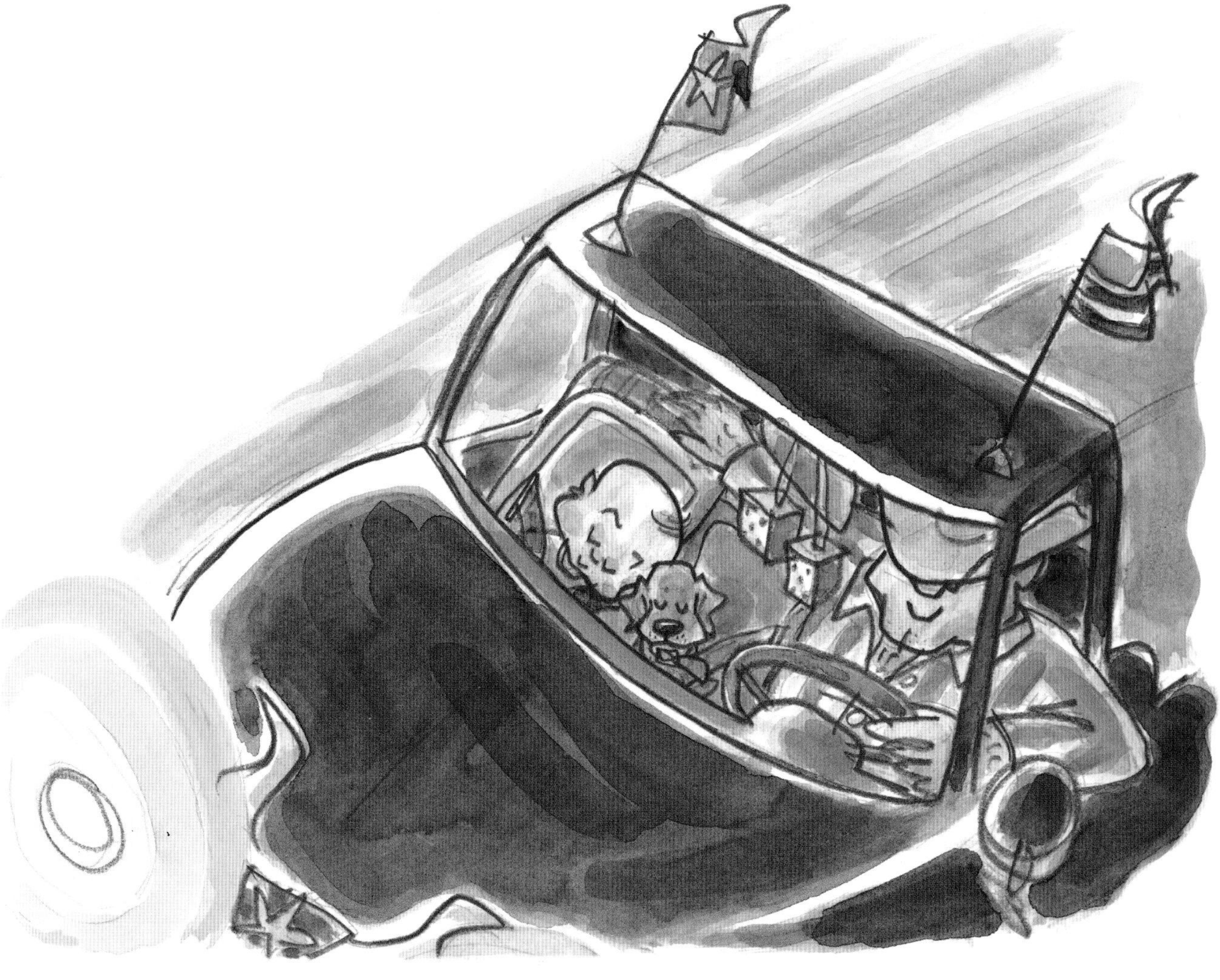

Night-night.